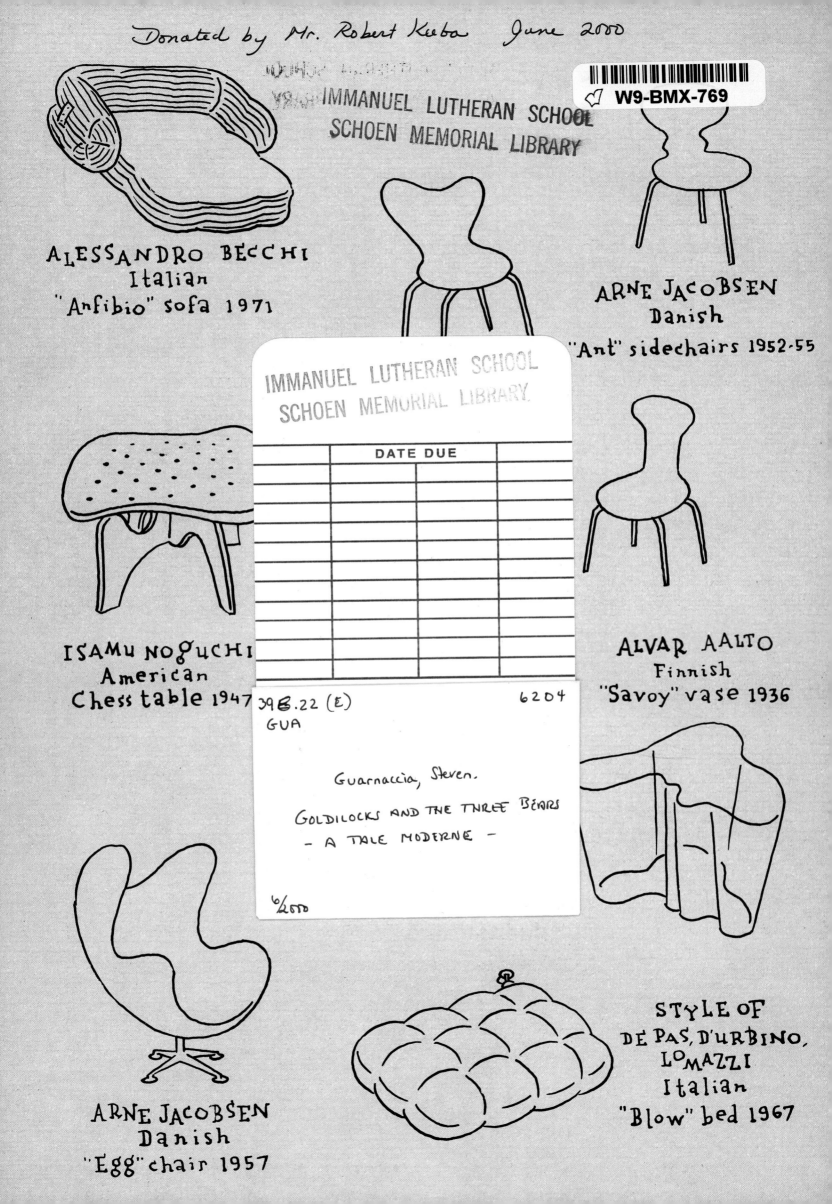

Donated by Mr. Robert Keeba   June 2000

W9-BMX-769

ALESSANDRO BECCHI
Italian
"Anfibio" sofa 1971

ARNE JACOBSEN
Danish
"Ant" sidechairs 1952-55

ISAMU NOGUCHI
American
Chess table 1947

ALVAR AALTO
Finnish
"Savoy" vase 1936

ARNE JACOBSEN
Danish
"Egg" chair 1957

STYLE OF
DE PAS, D'URBINO,
LOMAZZI
Italian
"Blow" bed 1967

To Joseph Eichler and Milton Miller,
two modernist uncles with great taste

Acknowledgments

I would like to thank Jacques Binsztok, Brigitte Morel, Howard Reeves, Feodor Rojankovsky, les Trois Ourses, Hugo Weinberg,
Lia Ronnen, Florence Barrau, Chris Gash, and Tamara Petrosino

Artist's Note

I use a brush and India ink to give the line a fat, luscious quality, and to allow me to vary the line from very thin to very thick.
I also use India ink to create the black background. On the black, I draw with an opaque, pastel-colored pen. I fill in areas—first
outlined in black—with Winsor & Newton watercolors, which I mix to achieve the palette I want.

Original handlettering by Steven Guarnaccia

Library of Congress Cataloging-in-Publication Data
Guarnaccia, Steven.
Goldilocks and the three bears / retold and illustrated by Steven Guarnaccia.
p.   cm.
Summary: Illustrations featuring elements of the modernism movement in art provide a new look to this traditional tale of the
uninvited visit of a young girl to the home of a family of bears. Includes a list of designers.
ISBN 0-8109-4139-2
[1. Bears Folklore. 2. Folklore.]   I. Goldilocks and the three bears. English.   II. Title.
PZ8.1.G933Go 2000
398.22—dc21   99–35493

Published in 2000 by Harry N. Abrams, Incorporated, New York

Printed and bound in Belgium

 Harry N. Abrams, Inc.
100 Fifth Avenue
New York, N.Y. 10011
www.abramsbooks.com

GOLDILOCKS and the THREE BEARS

A Tale Moderne

Retold and illustrated
by Steven Guarnaccia

Harry N. Abrams, Inc., Publishers

Once upon a time,
a family of bears
lived in a split-level
house deep in the forest.
There was a big burly Papa Bear,
a medium-sized Mama Bear, and
their pint-sized Baby Bear.

And in their house was a chair for each of them: a big burly chair for the Papa Bear, a medium-sized chair for the Mama Bear, and a pint-sized chair for the Baby Bear.

Upstairs they each had a bed.
There was a big burly bed for the
Papa Bear, a medium-sized bed for the
Mama Bear, and a pint-sized
bed for the Baby Bear.

One day, the Mama Bear
made chili for lunch.

There was a big burly bowl for
Papa Bear, a medium-sized bowl for
Mama Bear, and a pint-sized
bowl for the Baby Bear.

The chili was piping hot, so the bears decided to go for a ramble in the woods while it cooled down.

Before long, a little girl named
Goldilocks came to the bears' house
and rapped on the front door.
There was no answer, but as she
was a curious young girl, she
let herself in to look around.

Goldilocks immediately spied the three chairs. She climbed up into the big burly chair, but it was hard as a rock.

Next, she tried to get comfortable in the medium-sized chair, but it was way too soft.

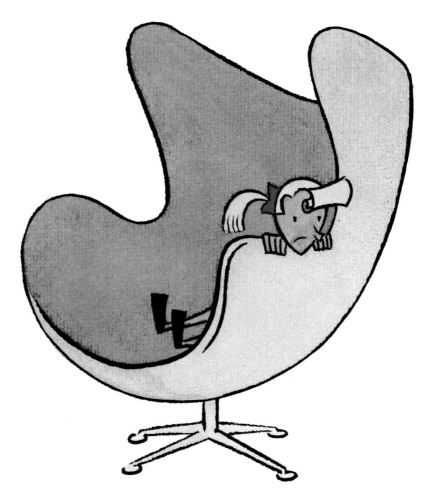

Finally, she tried the pint-sized chair, and it fit her perfectly. But just as she was getting cozy, the chair broke into pieces.

Before long, Goldilocks smelled the chili.
She realized how hungry she was, so she
tasted a spoonful from the big burly bowl.
It was so hot she burned her tongue. Then
she tried the chili in the medium-sized
bowl. It was too chilly.

But when she tasted the chili in
the pint-sized bowl, it was
just the way she liked it, and she
licked the bowl clean.

The warm food made Goldilocks
sleepy, so she went upstairs
to lie down.

First she tried the big burly bed, but it was too hard.

The medium-sized bed was too soft.

But when she lay down in the
pint-sized bed, it was just right,
and she fell asleep immediately.

Not long after, the bears,
done with their walk, made
their way home to eat lunch.

When Papa Bear entered the house,
he noticed something was wrong.
"Humph! Someone's been sitting in my
chair!" he said.

"Oh, fur and honey! Someone's been
sitting in my chair, too!" said Mama Bear.
"Oh, rats! Someone's been sitting in
my chair, and has smashed it to
smithereens!" said Baby Bear.

When Papa Bear sat down to eat,
he said with a gravelly growl, "Harumph!
Somebody's been eating my chili!"
Mama Bear looked at her bowl and the
spoon with chili on it.
"Someone's been eating my chili!" she said.
Baby Bear said, "It's so unfair, someone's
been eating my chili, and has
eaten it all up."

Now the three bears grumbled,

clattered, and bopped up the stairs.

"Grrr, someone's been sleeping in my bed!"
growled Papa Bear.
"Buzz Fuzz! Someone's been sleeping in
my bed," said Mama Bear.

"Gee Whillikers!" said Baby Bear.
"Someone's been sleeping in my bed,
and she's still there!"

Goldilocks woke with a start and saw
the three bears standing there, looking
down at her curiously.
"Yikes!" she said. Goldilocks bounced
out of Baby Bear's bed, down the stairs,
and out the door. She ran off towards
her home, and never set foot in that
part of the forest again.

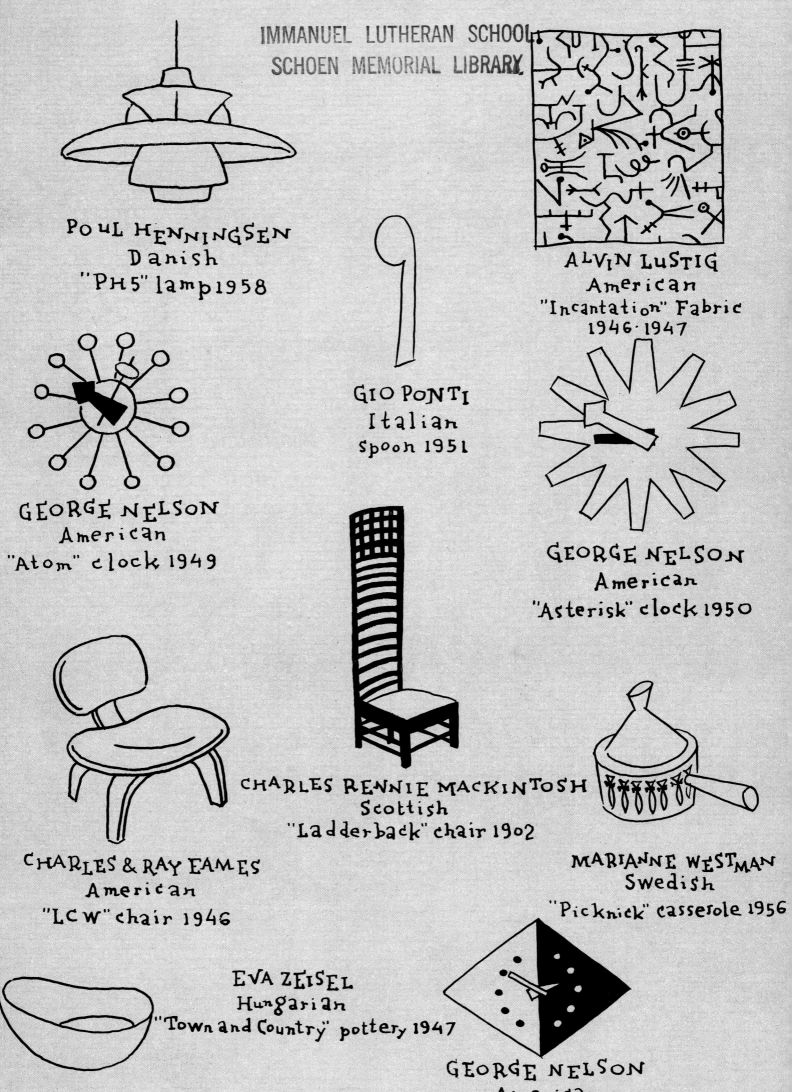

POUL HENNINGSEN
Danish
"PH5" lamp 1958

ALVIN LUSTIG
American
"Incantation" Fabric
1946-1947

GIO PONTI
Italian
Spoon 1951

GEORGE NELSON
American
"Atom" clock 1949

GEORGE NELSON
American
"Asterisk" clock 1950

CHARLES RENNIE MACKINTOSH
Scottish
"Ladderback" chair 1902

CHARLES & RAY EAMES
American
"LCW" chair 1946

MARIANNE WESTMAN
Swedish
"Picknick" casserole 1956

EVA ZEISEL
Hungarian
"Town and Country" pottery 1947

GEORGE NELSON
American
"Kite" clock 1953